# Dickens's Mittens

By Julia Williamson

**Dickens's Mittens** by Julia Williamson

ISBN  978-1-304-31235-8

# Dickens's Mittens

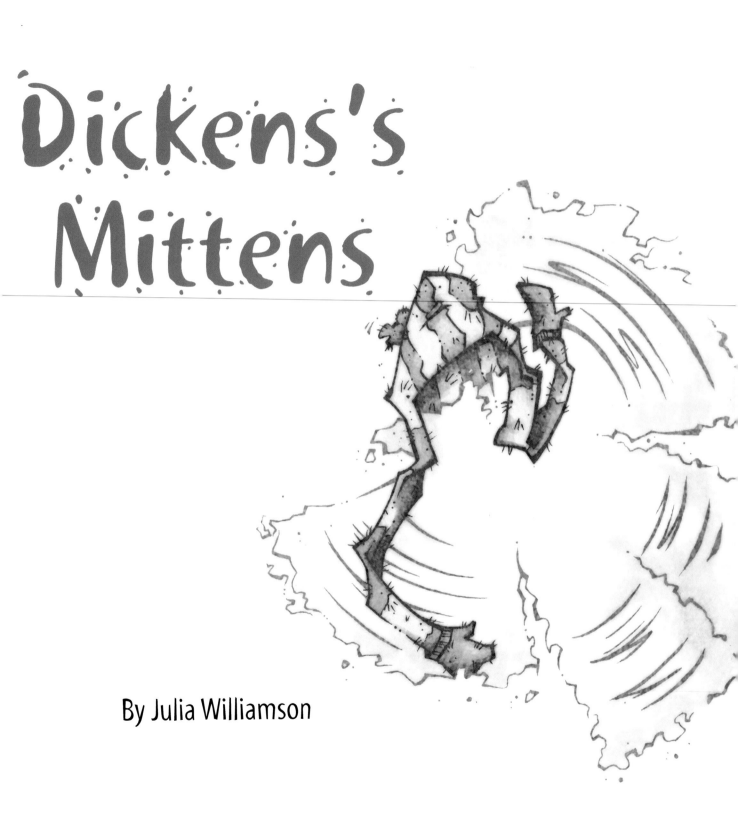

By Julia Williamson

I'd like you to meet my big brother Dickens.
He has a hard time keeping up with his mittens.
Mother sends him to school with two pairs, one and two.
But back home he returns with none. What to do?

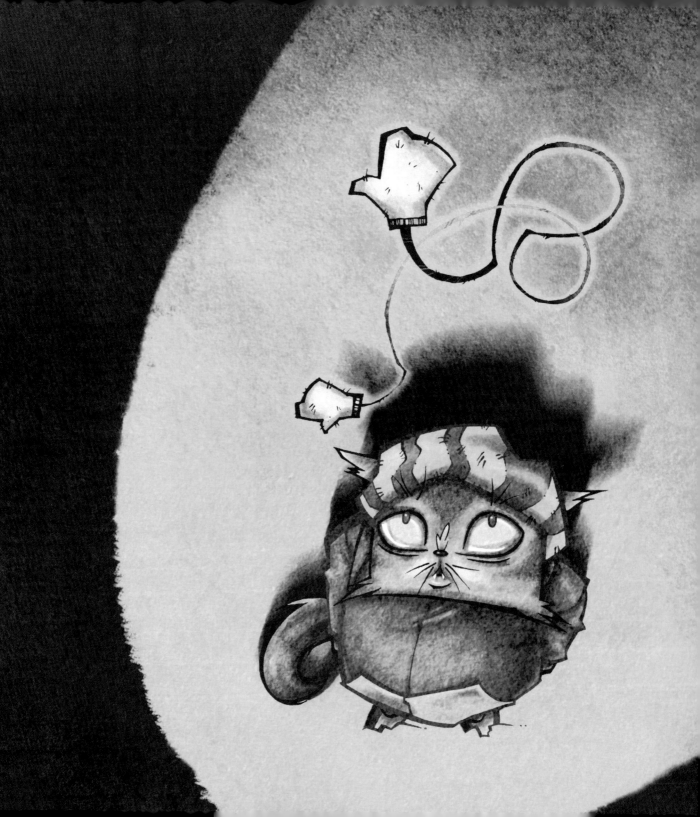

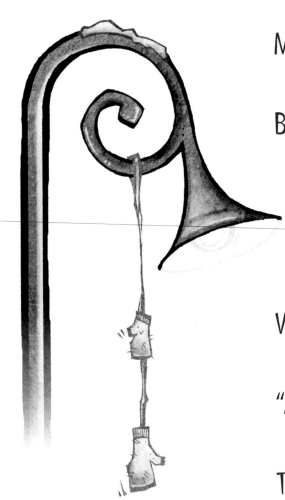

Mom tried fixing them to his
    coat sleeves with some string.
But again he returned without them.
    What a strange thing!

When asked what had happened
    my big brother cried,
"An alien ship came down
    from the sky!
They came down demanding
    my mittens so yellow.
And I handed them over
    like a scared little fellow!"

So once again Mother attached
   the two things,
This time with a scarf
   instead of the string.
Back home he returned
   without them, not one.
And when asked why,
   this is the new tale he begun...

"On my journey back home
   I passed by a castle.
A princess asked for my help,
   if it was no hassle.
So with my two mittens
   attached with your care,
I helped the fair maiden
   get down from up there."

Instead of string or a scarf,
  this time Mom used a hat.
But of course, don't you know,
  Dickens returned without that.

"A band of ice pirates
  tried to tie me up
Using the hat and mittens
  that you made with love.
But with my quick thinking
  and fast moving feet,
Back home I returned!
  Such a marvelous feat!"

Off to school the next day
    Dickens had in his pack
Not one or two pairs, but six!
    Imagine that!
Just like the days before,
    back home he returned
With no mittens at all!
    Something had to be learned!


The string did not work,
    nor the scarf, nor the hat.
Mom had to think of something,
    and it had to be fast!

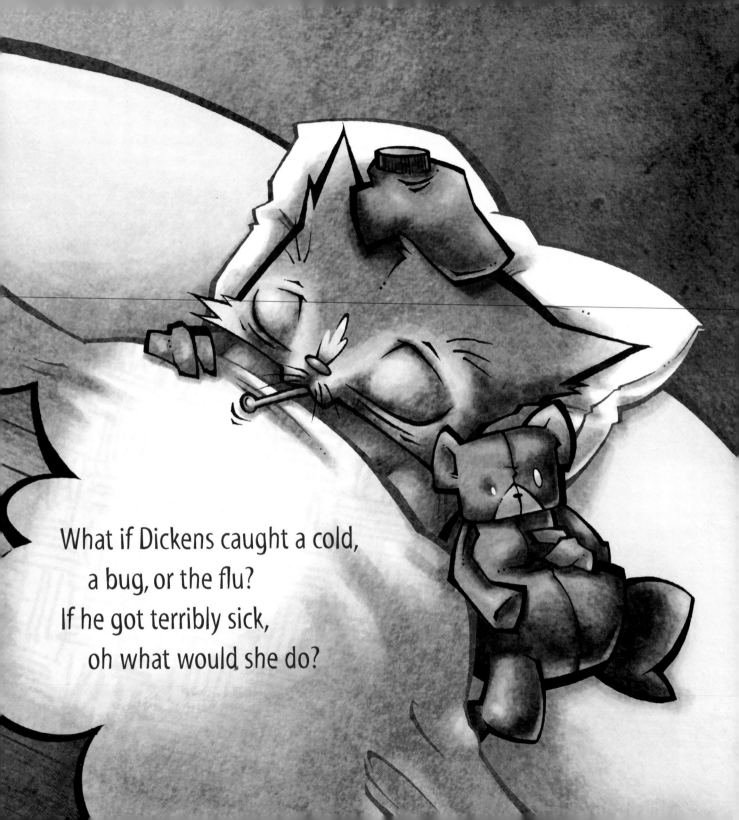

What if Dickens caught a cold,
a bug, or the flu?
If he got terribly sick,
oh what would she do?

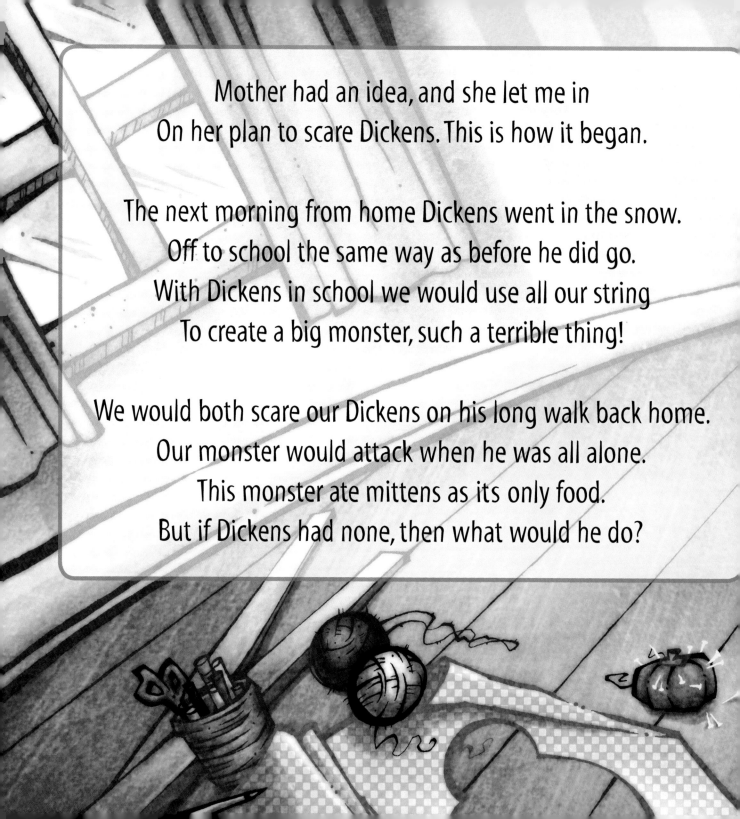

Mother had an idea, and she let me in
On her plan to scare Dickens. This is how it began.


The next morning from home Dickens went in the snow.
Off to school the same way as before he did go.
With Dickens in school we would use all our string
To create a big monster, such a terrible thing!


We would both scare our Dickens on his long walk back home.
Our monster would attack when he was all alone.
This monster ate mittens as its only food.
But if Dickens had none, then what would he do?

The plan worked out perfectly!
It worked like a charm!

"MITTENS!"
Screamed the monster!
Dickens screamed with alarm.

"You unhand my kitten!"
Mother yelled with a start.

"I MUST HAVE SOME MITTENS!"
Was my rehearsed part.

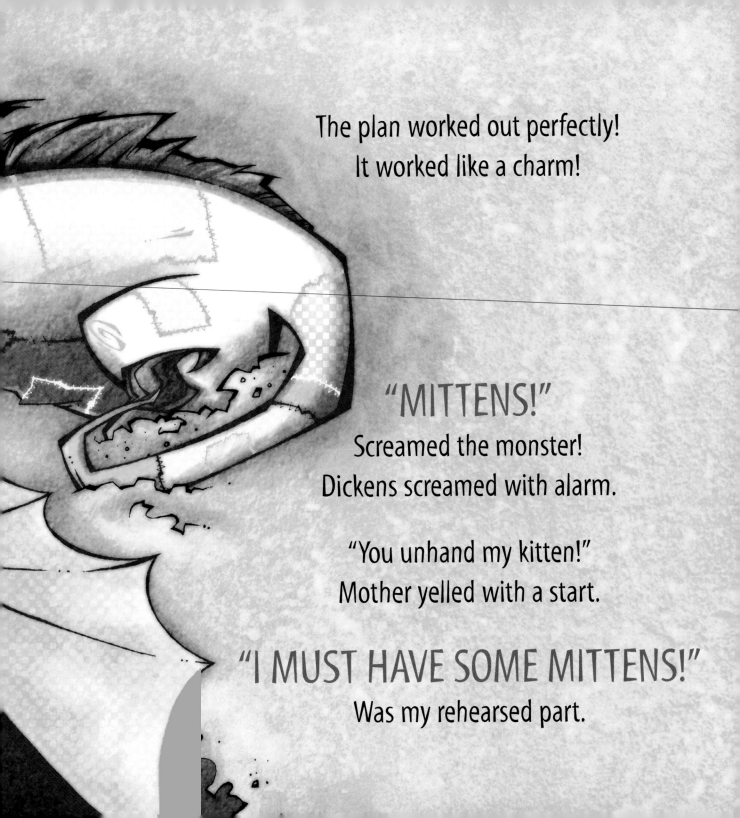

"Now listen here Dickens!" Our Mother did yell.
"You must do what I say. So listen up well!
I've made you these mittens
    with much love and care.
        As long as you wear them
            nothing can harm you. I swear!

You must put them on now,
    or this monster will eat them.
Once you have them on,
    then we can defeat him!"

As quick as a breeze
    Dickens put on those mittens
and inside he ran,
    such a scared little kitten!

Through the whole night
   with his mittens he slept.
And for the next three years
   those two mittens he kept!

Not a pair did he lose.
   Not ever again!
Mother and I smiled
   at our wonderful plan.
With her love and care
   she taught her sweet Dickens
The importance of taking
   good care of his mittens.

So if you are a kitten this big or this small,
Or maybe you are not a kitten at all.
No matter the monster, no matter the scare,
Nothing in the world can beat a mother's love and care!

In loving memory of my mother.